FIVE WAYS TO MAKE A FRIEND

FIVE WAYS TO MAKE A FRIEND

Gillian Cross

ILLUSTRATED BY
Sarah Horne

Barrington Stoke

First published in 2020 in Great Britain by
Barrington Stoke Ltd
18 Walker Street, Edinburgh, EH3 7LP

www.barringtonstoke.co.uk

Text © 2020 Gillian Cross
Illustrations © 2020 Sarah Horne

A CIP catalogue record for this book is available
from the British Library upon request

ISBN: 978-1-78112-908-1

Printed in China by Leo

Contents

Chapter 1

A New School – and No Friends

It was Ella's first day at her new school.

"You're going to love it here," said her dad as they walked into the playground. "This school is small and quiet – just like you."

Ella made herself smile. She was missing her old school and all her friends. But she didn't want Dad to know. It wasn't his fault that his job had made him move.

"Here we are!" said Dad. He pushed the school door open.

Ella couldn't believe how quiet it was inside. There was no one shouting or running along the corridor.

All the kids must be in their classrooms, she thought.

There was a teacher waiting for them. "Hello, Ella," she said. "I'm Mrs Brown. Come and meet your new class."

Dad kissed Ella goodbye. "Have a great day!" he said. Then he went off to work and Ella went along the corridor with Mrs Brown.

"It's not a very big class," Mrs Brown said. "There are ten boys and just four girls. You'll get to know them all very quickly." She pushed the classroom door open and in they went.

Ella saw the four girls right away. They were all sitting together at the back of the room, chatting.

When Ella walked in, they looked at her for a moment. Then they turned away and went on talking.

No one smiled at Ella except one of the boys at the front of the class.

Mrs Brown pointed at an empty chair next to him. "Sit with Josh for now," she said. "The girls will show you the rest of the school at break. Won't you, girls?"

One of the girls looked round. "What?" she said.

"Take Ella round the school at break," Mrs Brown said. "Show her where everything is."

"Oh. OK," said the girl, but she didn't look at Ella. She went on talking to the others while Mrs Brown called the register.

Ella sat down in the empty chair.

"Hi," said Josh softly. He was the boy who had smiled.

"Hello," Ella said back. She was thinking about the four girls. Were they going to be friendly when they took her round at break?

*

The girls were at the back of the class, but Ella heard them talking all morning. By the time it was break, she had worked out all their names. They were:

- Tanya, who had long blonde hair and a very loud laugh;

- Kara, who looked like a model;

- Rose, who was crazy about horses; and

- Daisy, the Top Girl, who bossed all the others around.

She remembered their names, but they didn't remember hers.

"Time to show Ella round the school," said Mrs Brown when the bell rang for break.

"Ella who?" said Tanya.

"I think it's the new girl," said Daisy. She nodded at Ella. "Come on then, new girl. Let's get going."

Daisy set off along the corridor with all the other girls behind her. They went so quickly Ella had to jog to keep up.

As they went, Daisy pointed at the rooms they passed. "That's the library," she said. "And the canteen. And the Head's office. And the gym ..."

Help! Ella thought. *She's going too fast. I'll never remember it all.* But she was too shy to ask Daisy to slow down.

They went round the whole school in five minutes.

Then Daisy said, "That's it. OK, new girl?"

She didn't wait for Ella to answer. She nodded at the other girls and they all ran out into the playground. Ella ran after them, but they didn't look back at her. For the rest of break, she saw them laughing and talking, but she was too shy to try to join in.

She just stood in a corner of the playground all on her own. It was horrible.

Chapter 2

The Perfect Book!

I need to try harder, Ella thought. *I have to show the other girls that I want to make friends. Maybe I can sit with them at lunch.*

At lunch-time, she looked round for the other girls. They were all sitting together, talking and giggling as they ate their lunch. Ella took her tray across to their table and sat down next to them.

"Hello," she said in a very small voice.

But the girls didn't even look up. They were making too much noise to hear her.

Ella was too unhappy to eat much. She had only eaten half her lunch when the other girls finished theirs. They jumped up and ran outside, and Ella was left looking at a plate full of cold pasta. She ate it very slowly, trying not to cry.

After she'd finished, there was still half an hour of lunch-time left. She didn't want to go outside. *No one will talk to me*, she thought. *It will be just like break.*

But where else could she go? For a moment, she couldn't think of anywhere. Then she had an idea. When the girls took her round at break, Daisy had pointed to the library. That would be a good place to go – if she could find it again.

Everyone had to be quiet in a library, so it wouldn't matter if no one talked to her. She could find a book and read until the end of lunch-time.

Ella tried to remember where it was. She went down the corridor and looked at all the doors. When she found the library, she pushed the door open and peeped in. There was no one there except Josh, the boy who sat next to her in class. He looked up and smiled at her when he saw her.

"Hi, Ella," he said. "Is everything going OK?"

"Oh. Yes. Yes," Ella said quickly. She didn't want him to know how unhappy she was. "I – um – I just came in to find a book to read."

"This is good." Josh showed her the book he was reading. "You could try the first book in this series. It's over there."

"Thanks," Ella said. "I'll have a look."

Josh went back to reading his book and Ella walked towards the shelf he'd pointed at. But before she got there, she saw something else.

A book called *Five Ways to Make a Friend*.

That was just what she needed! She pulled it off the shelf and sat down to read it.

"Got no friends?" said the book. "Try one of these five great ways to make new friends."

1. Bake some cakes to share with your friend-to-be.

2. Tell them when they've done something good.

3. Find a new hobby to make them interested in you.

4. Invite them to a party.

5. Save them when they're in danger.

There were lots of ways to make friends! Suddenly Ella felt very excited. She just had to pick one to try.

It didn't take her long to choose. She loved baking and everyone said her cakes were amazing. Tomorrow she was going to come to school with a big tin full of cakes!

*

No one spoke to Ella that afternoon, but she didn't care. *You'll talk to me tomorrow!* she thought. *When you taste my cakes!*

As soon as she got home, she told her dad what she wanted to do.

"Great." Dad smiled. "Save a cake for me!"

Ella spent the whole evening in the kitchen. She made pink cupcakes. And chocolate brownies. And a big carrot cake with lemon and sugar on the top. She gave Dad a cupcake and a brownie, but she wouldn't let him cut the carrot cake.

"That's for my friends at school," she said.

Dad grinned. "You've got friends already?" he said. "That's great!"

Ella grinned back. *I haven't got any friends yet*, she thought. *But I soon will have.*

*

Next day, Ella took all her cakes to school in a big tin. When it was time for break, she put the tin on her table and took off the lid.

"Look!" she said to Daisy and Tanya and Rose and Kara. "These are for you." She thought the girls would be happy and excited when they saw her beautiful cakes.

But everything went wrong.

Tanya looked into the tin and shook her head. Her long blonde hair swung round her face.

"Cake gives you spots!" she said.

"Yuck! Spots!" shouted all the other girls.

They didn't even look at Ella's cakes. They just shook their heads, like Tanya, and ran out of the room.

Ella almost cried. Her plan hadn't worked. And what was she going to do with all the cakes? She and Dad couldn't eat them all.

She was just going to put the lid back on the tin when she heard a soft voice behind her.

"Those look good!"

It was Josh. He nodded at the cakes. "Who made those?"

"I did," Ella said. "I thought the other girls would like them. But ..." She had to stop talking so she didn't burst into tears.

Josh smiled at her. "It's a good day for us then," he said. He turned round and called to the other boys. "Hey, everyone! Look what Ella's got! Cake!"

It was like magic. As soon as he said "Cake!" all the other boys came running to Ella's table. They grinned and shouted as they reached out to grab the cakes.

"Fantastic!"

"Amazing!"

"Three cheers for Ella!"

In less than a minute, almost all the cakes had gone. The boys grinned at Ella and then ran outside to play football. All except Josh.

He looked a bit nervous. "Was that OK?" he said. "I know the cakes were for the girls, but ... I just thought ... Was it OK for the boys to eat them?"

Ella nodded. "Yes, it was fine. Um, did you have one?"

Josh laughed. "I didn't get a chance. The other boys pushed me out of the way."

Ella picked up the tin and held it out. "Here you are. There are two brownies left."

"One for me and one for you," Josh said.

He and Ella ate the brownies together.

"You're a really good cook," said Josh. "I bet the other cakes were nice too."

"Thank you." Ella was so pleased she went pink.

She wanted to go on talking to Josh, but she couldn't. She had to go back to the library and have another look at *Five Ways to Make a Friend*. Her first plan hadn't been any good, but there were four more things to try.

One of them had to work!

Chapter 3

That's Amazing!

Ella went back to the library and found the book. The second idea on the list was: "Tell them when they've done something good."

What did that mean? She turned to Chapter Two to find out.

"Watch your friend-to-be," said the book. "Every time they do something good, smile and say, 'Well done!' or 'Amazing!' That will make them happy. And they will think you're a kind and friendly person."

That's easy, Ella thought. The classroom was small, so it wasn't hard to watch them. Who would be the first one to do something good? Daisy? Tanya? Rose? Or Kara? Whoever it was, Ella would be ready to say, "That's amazing!"

And she didn't have to wait till tomorrow. She could start straight after break. Maybe she would have a new friend by lunch-time!

*

At the end of break, Ella hurried back to the classroom. The other girls were already there, giggling and talking. Ella sat down in her place, watching them carefully.

Tanya looked round and saw her. "What are you staring at?" she said crossly.

"I ..." Ella thought fast. "I – um – I was just thinking how nice your hair looks."

Tanya looked cross. "No, it doesn't," she said. "It needs washing. Don't remind me!"

She turned back to the other girls and Ella heard them whispering about her. *I need to be more careful*, Ella thought. *It has to be something really good.*

Her chance came just before lunch. They were doing Maths and Mrs Brown had told Ella to sit next to Kara for this lesson. She had a quick look at Kara's book. Maybe she could say, "Kara! You're really good at Maths!"

But Kara wasn't doing Maths. She was drawing a picture of a girl with long hair in a prom dress. It was a really good picture. The girl looked beautiful.

"That's amazing!" whispered Ella.

She said it very softly, but Mrs Brown heard her voice and looked up. "What's going on over there?" she said.

"Nothing!" Kara said quickly.

But Mrs Brown was already coming over to them. Oh no! Ella didn't know what to do. Now Kara was going to get into trouble. And it was all her fault.

"What's the matter, Ella?" said Mrs Brown. "Is the Maths too hard for you?" She wasn't cross. In fact, she smiled kindly. Then she looked down at the table and her smile vanished. "What are you doing?" she said. "That's not Maths!"

Ella looked down too. There, right in front of her, was the picture of the girl in the prom dress. Kara must have pushed it across the table. Now it looked as if Ella had been drawing.

"It's not ..." Ella started to say. Then she stopped. If she said it wasn't her picture, Kara might get into trouble. *And then she won't be my friend*, Ella thought. So she shut her mouth and looked up at Mrs Brown without saying anything.

Mrs Brown shook her head. "Why are you drawing a picture in the Maths lesson, Ella?" she said. "You'll have to stay in at lunch-time to finish your work."

Ella felt terrible. Everyone was staring at her. But she didn't say anything. She just looked down at the table.

As Mrs Brown walked away, Kara whispered to Ella. "Thanks for not telling."

"That's OK," Ella muttered. She made herself smile, but she still felt upset. Now her second plan had gone wrong. Would she ever find a friend?

*

When Ella had eaten her lunch, she went back to the classroom. Mrs Brown was waiting for her with a worksheet.

"Do everything on the worksheet," she said. "Then you can go out to play – if there's any time left."

Ella took the worksheet and sat down at her table. She was just going to start when she saw a piece of paper on the table. "For Ella," it said. "Sorry you have to stay in." Ella picked up the paper. Underneath was a chocolate bar.

Someone had left it for her. Was it Kara?

Ella didn't know, but she suddenly felt much better. As she started the worksheet, she was smiling.

She wasn't going to give up trying to find a friend! There were five ideas in that book and she'd only tried two of them.

As soon as she'd finished the worksheet,
Ella went back to the library to see what was
next on the list. The third idea was: "Find a
new hobby to make them interested in you."

Right! That was what she was going to do!

Chapter 4

Ella's New Hobby

Ella spent the rest of the day thinking about hobbies. She had to find a hobby that wasn't too expensive. Something interesting. And something she could bring to school so people would see her doing it. But she didn't have much money, so it had to be really cheap.

Was there a hobby like that? She couldn't think of one.

Then something gave her an idea. At the end of the day, two of the boys started fooling about making paper darts. They kept throwing them at each other and then making new ones.

And all the darts were exactly the same.

Boring! Ella thought. *They ought to make different ones.*

She was sure there were lots of different darts you could make. She'd seen pictures of them. And not just darts. You could make all sorts of other things too. Just by folding paper.

You didn't need anything else. Only paper.

That's it! Ella thought. *That can be my new hobby!*

Ella hurried home to look on the computer. There must be a website that would show her how to make something better than darts. Then all she had to do was get some paper and practise folding it ...

She found lots of websites. Folding paper was called origami – and you could make beautiful things. Boxes and boats and birds. Flowers and butterflies and aeroplanes.

And dragons.

Ella really, really wanted to make a dragon. But that looked very hard. So she started with a boat. She made three boats and then tried a flower.

By bedtime, she could make boats and flowers – and little boxes too. And she could nearly make a butterfly. She loved her new hobby.

But she wasn't ready to take it to school yet. Not until she could make something amazing. Like a dragon. So she kept very quiet at school – and as soon as she got home, she practised. All Thursday evening. All Friday evening. And all over the weekend.

By Monday morning, she was ready. She put some squares of paper into her bag and smiled as she went off to school. She was going to surprise everyone!

*

Ella didn't say anything about her new hobby. When it was break, she just sat down in the playground and started folding paper. First she made a box. Then she made three flowers and then a little white bird. As she finished each one, she put it on the ground beside her.

She was just finishing a dragon when Daisy and the other girls came past. Ella looked up at them. "Hi," she said.

Daisy looked down. "Hi, Ella," she said. She looked at the flowers and the bird.

Tanya looked too. "What are those?" she said.

"I made them," Ella said. "It's my new hobby."

"Cool," said Kara. But she didn't sound interested.

Rose looked at the dragon Ella was making. "Is that a horse?" she said.

Ella shook her head. "No, it's a dragon."

"Can you make a horse?" Rose said.

"Not yet," said Ella.

"Boring!" said Rose. And she ran off with the other girls.

The girls didn't bother to look where they were going. They trod on all the things Ella had made. The paper box was squashed flat. The flowers got torn. And the little white bird blew away into a puddle.

Transit items (s)

Current time: 23/08/2021, 11:13
Item ID: C903268727
Title: Five ways to make a friend
Transit to: Strathfoyle Library
Transit to group: Full access to all libraries, Derry Group, FLOATING

Libraries NI

Everything was messed up. Except the dragon, because Ella was still holding that.

I won't cry, Ella thought. *I won't!*

She made herself go on with the dragon. As she folded the last little bit, a voice behind her said, "That's amazing."

She looked round. Josh was standing there looking down at the dragon.

"That's beautiful," he said. "I wish I could make one."

"It's not as hard as it looks," Ella said. "Want me to show you?"

Josh nodded and sat down next to her. Ella put down the dragon she had just finished and picked up a piece of blue paper. She gave Josh a yellow piece.

"OK," she said. "Now copy me."

She began folding and Josh copied her.

"You're being very careful," he said.

Ella nodded. "You have to get the folds just right or it doesn't work." She looked at the dragon Josh was making. "That's much better than my first one. But you need to move that fold a bit."

"Like this?" Josh said.

Ella smiled. "That's perfect."

By the end of break, Josh had made a dragon of his own. It was a bit wobbly and crooked, but he was very proud of it.

He showed it to Mrs Brown when they went back into the classroom. "Look at my dragon," he said. "Ella showed me how to do it."

Daisy and the other girls were right behind him. Ella watched them look quickly at Josh's dragon as he put it down on his table. *Maybe they are interested after all*, Ella thought. *Maybe it's time to try another idea for making friends!*

Mrs Brown smiled at Josh's dragon. "That's beautiful," she said. "I know! Let's write some dragon stories this afternoon."

Ella stopped feeling sad. She put her own dragons on the table in front of her, next to Josh's dragon. Then she started writing. But she wasn't really thinking about her story. She was thinking about *Five Ways to Make a Friend*.

What was the next idea in the book?

Chapter 5

Party Time!

The next idea in the book was much more difficult: "Invite them to a party".

She couldn't do that on her own. She'd have to get Dad to help her.

Ella waited until after tea, when she and Dad were doing the washing-up. When they'd nearly finished, she said, "Dad, can I have a party?"

"A party?" Dad looked surprised. "It's not your birthday."

"I know," Ella said. "But I'd like to ask some people to tea. Four girls."

"Four?" Dad said. "Yes, that's a party. When do you want to have it?"

Ella took a deep breath. "On Saturday."

"Saturday!" Dad dried his hands and sat down at the kitchen table. "We'd better make a plan right away then. Shall we make cakes?"

"No!" Ella almost shouted it. "They don't like cakes."

Dad looked surprised. "So who ate all those cakes you took to school last week?"

"That was the *boys*," Ella said. "I'm asking girls to my party."

"OK," Dad said. "So do they like pizza?"

Ella thought about what the other girls had for lunch. "Yes, pizza is good. And cheese. And fruit. And maybe some ice cream."

She and Dad made a long list of party food. When they'd finished, Dad looked at the list. "It's going to be a proper party," he said. "How about sending proper invitations?"

Ella clapped her hands. "Let's make them on the computer!" she said.

They spent the evening making invitation cards. Ella found a picture of a beautiful girl with long golden hair to go on the front. The girl was riding a horse and carrying a banner that said, "Top Girl!"

Inside, the card said:

You are invited to a party on Saturday

at Ella's house

Please come!

Dad and Ella put the cards into four envelopes and Ella wrote names on the front: Daisy, Tanya, Rose and Kara.

"Do you want to ask anyone else?" said Dad. "How about some of the boys?"

Ella shook her head. Daisy never talked to any of the boys. Nor did Tanya or Rose or Kara. "This is a party for girls," she said.

*

When Ella got to school the next day, she put the cards in the other girls' places. Daisy came in first. She opened the envelope and looked at the card.

"A party?" she said. "Is it your birthday, Ella?"

Ella shook her head. "I just wanted a party. And there's going to be pizza and fruit and ice cream – and no cake!"

"Yay!" said Daisy. She tossed the invitation into her bag and looked round as Tanya and Kara came in. "Hey, everyone. Ella's having a party on Saturday."

Josh was just behind the girls. He must have heard about the party and Ella wished she could ask him too. But how could she? What would the other girls say?

"A party?" said Tanya.

"Cool," said Kara. "Thanks for inviting us."

Daisy nodded. "We love pizza!"

Ella looked round. "Where's Rose?" she said. "I've got an invitation for her too."

"She's got a cold," said Daisy. "I'll take her invitation round to her house." She put Rose's envelope into her bag too.

*

"Well?" said Dad when Ella got home after school. "Are they coming to your party?"

Ella nodded. She was very excited. "They all said they love pizza. But Rose wasn't there, because she's got a cold. Daisy's taking her card round to her house."

"If Rose has only got a cold, she'll be better by Saturday," said Dad. "I'd better make sure we have lots of pizza! I'll go to the shops tomorrow."

Chapter 6

Disaster!

Rose was away from school for the next three days. She came back on Friday morning. Ella saw her in the playground with the other girls and she ran over to talk to her.

"Are you coming to my party, Rose?" she said.

"Party?" Rose said, as if she didn't know what Ella was talking about.

"You know," said Daisy. "I gave your mum the invitation when you were ill."

"Oh, that!" Rose said. She shook her head. "No, I can't go to that. It's the horse show tomorrow."

"The horse show?" gasped Daisy.

Kara screamed, "Tomorrow? We thought it was next week."

"No, it's tomorrow," Rose said. She looked annoyed. "Aren't you coming?"

"Of course we are!" said Tanya. Daisy and Kara nodded.

"We always come!" Kara said.

Ella looked at them all. "But – but what about my party?"

The girls shook their heads. "Sorry," said Daisy. "We can't come. No way! We have to go and cheer for Rose at the horse show."

"We always go to watch her ride," said
Tanya and Kara.

The four girls linked arms and walked
across the playground, leaving Ella standing
all on her own. She didn't know what to do.
She'd have to tell Dad no one was coming to her
party. What about all the pizzas he'd bought?
And the ice cream?

Ella wanted to scream, but, if she did,
everyone would look at her. She closed her
eyes and stood very still in the middle of the
playground.

When she opened her eyes again, Josh was
standing next to her.

"Are you OK?" he said.

Ella tried to smile, but she couldn't. "I'm
having a party tomorrow," she told him. "But
no one's coming. And my dad's bought loads of

pizzas and ice cream. We'll never eat them all by ourselves."

Josh was quiet for a moment. Then he said, "I like pizza and ice cream." He grinned. "But not on the same plate."

Ella laughed. "You could have two plates," she said. She thought about all the pizza and ice cream. "You can come if you like," she said.

Josh thought for a moment. Then he nodded. "OK. What time?"

"Four o'clock," Ella said.

*

Ella didn't think it would be like a real party with just two of them. But she was wrong. They had a fantastic time. They started out by eating lots of pizza. Dad told some of his terrible jokes and Ella and Josh groaned and laughed.

Then Josh said, "Have you got any more paper, Ella? We could make Dragon Land."

Ella fetched the paper and they made lots of dragons. Josh's were yellow and Ella's were blue and they had dens made of pillows and blankets. Ella made her dragons fly round the room. Josh made a treasure heap for his dragons to sit on.

At first, the dragons had a fight. Then they made friends and Dad came in and said, "Time for ice cream."

Ella and Josh sat on the floor eating their ice cream.

"That was a good game," Ella said. "I'm glad the dragons made friends. I wish it was that easy to make friends with people."

"It is easy," Josh said.

Ella shook her head. "No, it's hard," she said. "I've tried everything in the book, but nothing works."

"What book?" said Josh.

"It's called *Five Ways to Make a Friend*," said Ella. She told him about it. And all the things she'd tried to make friends with the other girls. "There's only one thing left now," she said. "And it's not something I can plan."

"What is it?" said Josh.

"I have to save them when they're in danger," Ella said. "How can I do that unless there actually is some danger?"

Josh looked thoughtful. "You need to be in the right place at the right time," he said.

Ella didn't understand. "What do you mean?" she said.

"Well, nothing dangerous is going to happen at school," said Josh. "If you want to save the girls, it has to be outside."

Ella frowned. "But I never see them outside school."

"You could walk home with them," said Josh. "Something dangerous might happen in the street."

"Like what?" said Ella.

Before Josh could answer, there was a ring on the doorbell. His mum had come to fetch him and he had to go home. Ella was left on her own, thinking about what he had said.

She didn't really think there would be any danger in the street. But she and Daisy went home the same way. *I might as well try walking with her*, Ella thought.

It was the only idea she had left.

Chapter 7

Danger!

On Monday, Ella came out of school with Daisy. "Can I walk home with you?" she asked.

Daisy gave a shrug. "If you like," she said.

It wasn't much fun. As soon as they left school, Daisy put her headphones on. She started listening to her music and she hummed and jiggled as they walked. Ella tried talking, but Daisy couldn't hear anything she said.

When they were halfway home, there was a shout from behind them. "Watch out!"

Ella looked round. It was Josh, coming down the hill on his bike. He was going very fast.

"Hi, Josh!" Ella called.

"Watch out!" Josh yelled again. "My brakes aren't working!"

His bike was going faster and faster. And it was heading straight for Daisy and Ella!

"Get out of the way!" Josh yelled.

Ella jumped back, but Daisy didn't take any notice. She just went on humming and jiggling.

She can't hear! Ella thought. *She's going to get hurt!*

"Out of the way!!!" Josh shouted again.

Ella ran back and grabbed Daisy's arm, dragging her away from the road. A second later, Josh's bike whizzed past – just missing them both!

Daisy saw that. She gasped and took her headphones off. "He nearly crashed into me!" she said. "You saved me, Ella!"

"It was nothing," Ella said. "I just heard Josh shouting. I hope he hasn't hurt himself." She looked down the road, but she couldn't see him. He'd vanished round the corner.

"Never mind Josh," Daisy said. "You're a hero, Ella! Do you want to come to my sleepover on Saturday?"

"I ..." Ella was too surprised to speak.

"Tanya will be there," Daisy said with a big friendly smile. "And Rose and Kara. Do come!"

"Thank you," Ella gasped. "I'll ask my dad as soon as I get home."

She was very excited. But she couldn't help thinking about Josh. His bike had been going very fast. Had he crashed when he zoomed round the corner?

"I have to go," she said to Daisy. "See you tomorrow."

Ella ran the rest of the way down the hill. As soon as she went round the corner, she saw Josh just a little way ahead, pushing his bike. She ran to catch him up.

"Josh!" she said. "Are you OK?"

"I'm fine," Josh said. And he got back on the bike.

Ella grabbed his arm. "You can't ride that! Not if the brakes aren't working."

"It's OK," Josh said. "They're fine." He looked at Ella. "Did it work? Is Daisy your friend now?"

Did what work? Ella didn't understand. But she was too happy to care. "It's amazing!" she said. "I'm going to Daisy's sleepover on Saturday. Isn't that wonderful?"

She grinned at Josh. But he didn't grin back. He just gave a little nod and cycled away.

Chapter 8

The Sleepover

When Ella got home, she ran into the house. "Dad! Dad!" she shouted. "Can I go to Daisy's sleepover on Saturday?"

Dad grinned. "Of course you can," he said. "But you need some new pyjamas. Let's go shopping on Saturday morning."

*

Dad bought Ella a new pink onesie and some fluffy white slippers. When Ella got to Daisy's house, the other girls were already there. They all hugged Ella.

"Well done for saving Daisy," said Tanya.

"Great slippers!" said Rose.

"Can I try them on?" said Kara.

They all took their duvets into the sitting room and spread them out on the floor.

"I've got some great movies for us to watch," Daisy said. "We're having chips with the first one."

"Yay!" said Tanya.

"And pizzas with the second one," Daisy said.

Rose grinned. "Perfect!" she said.

"And with the third one – ice cream and chocolate bars!" yelled Daisy.

"Amazing!" shouted Kara.

Daisy's mum brought in the chips and they all settled down to watch the first movie.

At first, Ella had a great time. The movie was funny and the chips were great. But after half an hour, she started to get bored.

No one was talking. All the other girls just sat staring at the screen and eating chips. When Ella tried to talk, they all said, "Ssh!!"

It wasn't fun at all. It was ... boring.

Maybe it will get better when the movie's over, Ella thought.

But it didn't. Daisy just put on another movie. And the other girls kept staring at the screen, the way they had before. Except this time they were eating pizza.

Ella yawned. She was too full of chips to eat any pizza. And she was bored with watching movies. *I wish we were doing something*, she thought. *Like making dragons – the way I did with Josh.*

But she didn't dare say anything. And she was starting to feel sleepy. *Maybe I'll snuggle under my duvet for a bit*, she thought. *Maybe I'll just close my eyes ...*

Ten seconds later, she was fast asleep.

*

When Ella woke up, it was morning. She sat up and rubbed her eyes. All the other girls were lying around her, fast asleep.

Daisy's mother opened the door. "Hello, Ella," she said. "You missed the ice cream and chocolate last night. Do you want some for breakfast?"

"No, thank you," Ella said. She just wanted to go home. But she knew she couldn't leave yet.

Daisy's mother grinned and looked round the room. "Wake up, girls! It's breakfast time!"

The other girls started yawning and sitting up.

"I'm so tired!" groaned Daisy.

Rose rubbed her eyes and Kara started to brush her hair.

"I feel sick," said Tanya. "I ate too many chocolate bars last night."

"Me too," Daisy said. And Rose and Kara nodded.

Suddenly Ella remembered the other chocolate bar – the one she had found on her table at school. "Hey," she said. "Thanks for the chocolate bar you left me. When I had to stay in and do Maths. Was that you, Kara?"

"What?" said Kara. "No, it wasn't me."

All the other girls stared at Ella. She could see they didn't know what she was talking about. "There was a note on top," she said. "Saying 'For Ella'."

"Oh, I saw that!" said Kara. "Josh put it there. But I didn't know there was chocolate underneath."

Josh???

Ella's mouth dropped open. Josh had done that? She started remembering all the other nice things he'd done for her.

He made sure the cakes she'd baked weren't wasted.

He'd joined in with her new hobby, origami.

He'd come to her party and made Dragon Land.

And ... of course! Josh had only been pretending that his brakes weren't working so Ella could rescue Daisy.

I don't need to make a friend, Ella thought. *I've got one already!*

She smiled at the other girls as she ate her breakfast. It didn't matter what they thought about her. She would see her real friend at school on Monday.

They could talk about Dragon Land. And make some more origami. And at the weekend, maybe Josh could come to her house and help her bake cakes. And ...

Ella's head was buzzing with ideas. *We could write a book!* she thought. *We could call it* Fifty-Five Things to Do with a Friend!